For the past few years Rebecca Sparrow has been a weekly columnist at mamamia.com.au. Her first novel, *The Girl Most Likely* (2003), is in development to become a feature film. Her second, *The Year Nick McGowan Came to Stay* (2006), debuted as a stage play in 2007. Her most recent book, *Find Your Feet (the 8 things I wish I'd known before I left high school)* (2013), is the companion guide to the bestselling *Find Your Tribe (and 9 Other Things I Wish I'd Known in High School)* (2009). Rebecca is an ambassador for GIVIT: Goods for Good Causes and The Pyjama Foundation. She lives in Brisbane with her family. You can find Bec wasting time on Facebook at Rebecca Sparrow Online or at www.rebeccasparrow.com

Also by Rebecca Sparrow

The Girl Most Likely

The Year Nick McGowan Came to Stay

Find Your Feet (the 8 things I wish I'd known before I left high school)

Ask Me Anything (heartfelt answers to 64 anonymous questions from teenage girls)

find your tribe

(and 9 other things I wish I'd known in high school)

rebecca sparrow

UQP

First published 2010 by University of Queensland Press
PO Box 6042, St Lucia, Queensland 4067 Australia
Reprinted 2010, 2013, 2016 (twice)

www.uqp.com.au

Typeset in 11.25/17.5pt Legacy Serif by Jo Hunt, Victoria
Illustration by Chris Bellamy
Printed in Australia by McPherson's Printing Group, Victoria

The University of Queensland Press uses papers that are natural, renewable and recyclable products made from wood grown in sustainable forests. The logging and manufacturing processes conform to the environmental regulations of the country of origin.

Cataloguing-in-Publication Data
National Library of Australia

Sparrow, Rebecca, 1972-

Find your tribe : and nine other things I wish I'd known in high school / Rebecca Sparrow.

978 0 7022 3772 0 (pbk.)
978 0 7022 3794 2 (pdf.)

Girls--Conduct of life--Humor.
Girls--Life skills guides--Humor.
High school girls--Humor.
Teenage girls--Humor.

646.7008352

Contents

For Ava
who is so very loved
and inspired this book
in the first place

When I was in high school ...

The truth is, despite having written a novel entitled *The Girl Most Likely* – I wasn't. I wasn't the girl most likely to succeed in high school. I wasn't a prefect. I didn't win any awards in my final year. Not a single one. In fact, in high school, I was fairly average. I got pretty good grades, I guess, but I didn't top any subjects. And I certainly didn't stand out. Although when I look back at photos of me at seventeen I'm not entirely sure how I DIDN'T stand out considering that I looked like Harold Bishop with a perm (turn to page 122 for proof).

And while we're being honest, let's just say that high school also handed me some of my most crushing moments. Yep. Nobody invited me to my school formal. A guy that I was madly in love with barely knew I even existed. I was so bad at maths I ended up having to do Maths in Society (where the maths-challenged kids learn how to turn on a calculator). And despite the fact that I'd been playing netball since I was nine, I wasn't even chosen for the C-grade team in high school. Talk about a blow to the ego.

But here's the weird bit. Despite all that rotten stuff, I loved high school. Yep. Loved it. I'm one of those people who can actually, genuinely say they enjoyed it. A number of my closest friends today are the people I whispered secrets to during modern history and French and drama (and, clearly, PE and maths). I'm beginning to suspect that my grades would've been better if I'd actually shut up and paid attention in class.

Regardless of whether you hate the school, the teachers, the uniform, the subject choices or the quality of the lamingtons they serve at the tuckshop, high school gives you the chance to form some amazing new friendships and create memories you will hold close to your heart for many years to come. I had a great time hanging out with my friends, hatching plans to get boys to notice us and being in a number of school plays – and a not-so-great time analysing *Hamlet* to the point I wanted to vomit. (The guy was insane, can't we just accept it and move on?)

Does that mean you're meant to love every day of school? Nope. As with everything in life, there are guaranteed to be blah days when your hair, your homework or your clothes just don't sit right. There will be days when your favourite teacher tells you off. When the person you have a crush on fails to notice you even exist. When your best friend behaves more like your worst enemy. And when even the C-grade netball team thinks you'd be a dead weight and have the defending skills of a stapler.

But if you approach high school in the right way, if you go in each day with a bit of wisdom, with a few smarts up your sleeve, with the right attitude, then high school doesn't have to be completely and utterly horrendous. Arm yourself with some strategies and when a sucky day or week shows up you'll know how to handle it. You may even enjoy the journey!

So, here's a list of the things I've worked out that you need to know about not just surviving high school, but actually enjoying it. Some of these lessons I knew. Many of them I didn't. But best of all, they also apply to surviving life.

1 Find your tribe

Happiness in high school, I believe, is determined by two things: having fabulous, inspiring teachers and having great friends. Now unfortunately the 'fabulous, inspiring teachers' thing isn't something you can control. But if you're lucky enough to have a few fab teachers in high school who challenge and inspire you, who make you want to be in their classroom even on a Friday at two o'clock and who can still join in a conversation on your total addiction to Netflix, then count yourself extremely lucky.

The other major factor that will determine the quality of your time at high school is who you hang around. Your friends. And this is the bit you *can* control.

I'm going to cut to the chase. Life is too short to hang around with bitchy, negative people. So don't. In high school you want to surround yourself with people who 'get you'. You know, people who get your sense of humour and think you're funny. (Well, most of the time – maybe not when you're trying to see how many Tiny Teddies you can fit in your mouth!) True friends are those who support your dreams, cheer you on and are prepared to do CPR on you when you start choking on those Tiny Teddies. They provide a soft place for you to fall and are there to comfort you (and eat cookies'n'cream ice-cream with you when you're blue). Real friends don't slag you off the moment your back is turned or routinely put you down or humiliate you in front of others. Real friends don't leave you out. Instead, real friends 'have your back'. In other words, they're fiercely loyal and protective. My friend Franny describes finding real friends as finding your 'tribe' which I think is the perfect way to describe it. Your tribe is made up of people who you click with. People you can trust. People who see the world the way you see it.

People who like the same things as you. So choose friends at school who are from your tribe and high school will be *waaaaay* more enjoyable.

All friendships have ups and downs and, for whatever reason, girls can be incredibly bitchy to one another for no apparent reason. But when you've got great friends these little spats will last for maybe a day. Not weeks. Not months. And then you'll make up and want to get together again to plot a way for that hottie who catches your bus to finally notice you.

You know what else? You don't need to be in the cool group to enjoy high school. Aim to be someone who is friends with all different kinds of people at school. Rosalind Wiseman, author of *Queen Bees and Wannabes* calls this being a 'floater'. Floaters do their own thing, have high self-esteem and they definitely don't pay attention to peer pressure. Be authentic in your tastes. In other words, be who you are. Don't change your personality or your interests or your taste just to hang around with girls who spend all their time bitching and making fun of other people.

All this sounds obvious, right? And yet many adults will tell you it took them years (and some painful friendship experiences) to finally get this lesson. For some reason, many of us spend our spare time with snarky, negative people who make us feel worthless.

And don't think for a second that hanging around with the cool group will make you seem more attractive. There's nothing attractive about someone who behaves like a sheep and follows a leader. You're way better off hanging around with your tribe. After all, what is attractive is a girl who is confident, who can laugh at herself, who smiles a lot and who exudes a generous spirit.

While we're talking about friendship, let me just say that part of having good friends is being a good friend. Stop rolling your eyes, it's true. Don't bitch. Don't be the big mouth spreading rumours. Defend your tribe when others are trying to tear them down.

Two tribes are better than one ...

If possible, try and have a second group of friends or even just one great friend outside of school. Maybe you do a drama class on weekends, play a sport, are President of the

People Who Hate People Who Can't Differentiate Between You're and Your Society, are part of a youth group, Girl Guides, yodelling. Whatever. The point is sometimes when your school friends are driving you up the wall with their Ed Sheeran obsession, it's good to have another friend or friends outside of school that you can turn to and hang out with.

In short: hang with your tribe.

> *The key is to keep company with people who uplift you, whose presence calls forth your best.*
>
> **Epictetus, Greek philosopher**

A word on bullying ...

Bullying has always been around but now, thanks in part to mobiles and the internet, it's no longer an issue confined to school hours. Today, bullying continues around the clock and follows you into your home via cyberspace and text messaging. This book could be filled up just on the issue of bullying alone, but here are some things you should know ...

Bullying comes in many forms. It can be physical – where other girls or guys are beating you up or threatening to beat you up. It can be cyber bullying – where people are texting or emailing threats or horrible messages to you or about you to others or even spreading rumours or saying hurtful things on websites. Or it can be relational bullying – which includes stuff like being frozen out, having another student or a group of students refuse to make eye contact with you, making faces or noises behind your back and generally trying to make you feel excluded.

If you are being bullied, the most important thing to do is to TELL someone. Tell your parent or guardian.

Tell a teacher. And keep telling until someone DOES something about it. Most forms of bullying are actually illegal and the police can charge the bully with an offence. Don't be afraid to speak out. The only way things can change is if you tell someone about it. Don't suffer in silence.

This is why choosing the right group of friends at school is so important. You need to have a support network (or even just one true friend) who is there for you and whom you can trust.

If bullying is an issue for you, turn to page 118 for websites, help lines and books which will give you all the support you need. But most of all – tell somebody about it.

★ ★ ★ ★

If you're the one doing the bullying – think twice about it. Apart from being incredibly hurtful, the police are now able to charge teenagers with harassment. If you get a criminal record you can kiss goodbye certain careers.

When I was in high school I wish I'd known that being in the cool group would not equate to any form of real success in the real world! I was always a bit of a loner and definitely not in the cool group. In the end I was proud not to be – the majority of those girls were pretty nasty (to me and others) and spent a lot of time focusing on completely insignificant stuff. I have since seen a few of these girls as women and now that I am lucky and blessed to be successful at what I do, I am suddenly 'cool' to them. What a turnaround!

Katie Noonan, singer/composer

When I was in high school I was bullied over MSN ... I'm no expert but my motto was to think about the fact that high school is a very small portion of your life and once you get out, there is a whole entire universe out there. Once you realise that, you can spend your downtime picking up an instrument, playing sport or just working on yourself as a human being to make sure that you become an amazing person out of that situation. After all, success is the best revenge.

Ruby Rose, MTV VJ

For a long time as a teenager I was driven by what other people thought of me. I really cared about how I was perceived by others, whether they liked me or not. If I thought somebody didn't like me, it would just devastate me. What a waste of time – especially since some of the people I was so concerned about were people I didn't even particularly like! What I've learnt along the way is that there will always be people who don't like you – and there's absolutely nothing you can do about it. Just as there are people you won't necessarily like, even if you are not sure why. It's part of life, it's inevitable and it's absolutely fine. Instead of dwelling on the people you think don't like you, concentrate on the ones you know do!

Frances Whiting, journalist

2 Learn to bounce back

Life is wonderful and joyous and thrilling. It really is. But it can also be really, really hard. So here's one thing I know for sure – you are guaranteed to have some disappointments. You'll miss out on sporting teams or won't be chosen for a school play. You'll fail at stuff. You'll embarrass yourself. (I once set my fake fingernails on fire while working as a party hostess and lighting a birthday cake for a kid at McDonalds.) You, yes YOU, are destined to make some super-sized mistakes. And even when you're not making mistakes and life seems just peachy, out of the blue you'll still be hit with some pretty major disappointments.

This is where resilience comes into it. Success in life is all about being resilient and persistent. In other words, being able to get back up and keep going after you've been knocked down. Everyone falls down at some point. You, me, your English teacher, that hottie who sits near you on the bus. It's the people who are able to dust themselves off and keep going, who don't lose faith in their goals, who know that even after failing their driver's licence test twice that they are destined to be behind the wheel, who are the ones that will succeed.

It's important to know that people aren't born resilient. It's something you learn. A way to behave. So that's what you need to start doing, acting like someone who is resilient.

Resilient people ...

* know that failure and disappointment in life are normal
* don't give up easily

* let themselves feel sad when something goes wrong but after a day or two they try to learn from the failure and keep chasing their dream
* try to find the positive in bad situations
* are open to hearing feedback, advice or constructive criticism on better, smarter ways they can achieve their goals
* believe they have a lot to offer and know that mistakes and failures don't define who they are.

When you've got the blues

When you're dealing with disappointment (trying to heal a broken heart or sticky-tape your self-confidence back together), be extra kind to yourself. My friend Anna believes that being creative is always a fabulous remedy for the blues. Draw. Paint. Decorate a bag with buttons and ribbons. Make a batch of lemon cupcakes. Compose a poem or a song or a story. Being creative can help reignite a bit of your inner sparkle. For inspiration, go to www.meetmeatmikes.com – it's a wonderful, magical website which might just inspire you to make some cool bits and pieces. And then you could even sell them on www.madeit.com.au (that's a site for people to sell handmade things).

But maybe you feel about as creative as a ham sandwich right now. That's okay. Take time to curl up with your favourite novel (the one you've read a hundred times before) or your favourite movie or listen to some of your favourite music.

Here's what I go for (be warned, it's seriously uncool). I watch *Anne of Green Gables* or *The Goodbye Girl* or *Barefoot In the Park*. I read *The Book Thief* by Markus Zusak or *Bird by Bird* a non-fiction book by Anne Lamott (it's a book about writing but it makes me laugh out loud). As for music, I love Ryan Adams' *Gold* album.

What else could you do? Go for a walk in the sunshine with your friends, hang out at some Farmers' Markets (and taste test all the fresh food!) or do some volunteer work. Just know that you'll get through this phase and bounce back.

What if you can't bounce back?

In the classic 1960s movie *Breakfast at Tiffany's,* the main character Holly Golightly called it the mean reds – that's the type of depression that goes way beyond just having the blues. Depression is an issue that impacts two million Australian teenagers and adults. While it's completely normal to have a few down days over a major disappointment, if you still can't shake your sadness after a few weeks, that's a sign you need to talk to somebody.

Maybe sadness and depression isn't your problem. Maybe you're feeling stressed, nervous or scared about stuff that never used to bother you before. Or maybe you've started having panic attacks whenever you have to do an exam. If you notice any of these things happening, they're also a sign you need to talk to someone. Sometimes just one session with a school counsellor will have you back on track. At other times it might take some visits to a qualified psychologist. If all that freaks you out a bit, start by talking to an adult you trust. Just know that you don't have to feel rotten – there are lots of counselling services, medications, websites and support networks there to help you. Turn to page 118 to get you started.

The silver lining to screw ups

Nobody likes to make mistakes but, sometimes, screwing up is the best thing that can happen. Mistakes are how we learn what not to do. They teach us. Make us wiser. More savvy.

With mistakes comes a greater determination to succeed. You get wise pretty quickly. (Note to self: get rid of fake fingernails when working as a party hostess.) It makes you more empathetic to others. And somehow, it moves you forward even though at the time it doesn't feel like it. Just try your best not to repeat the mistake. Maybe that means getting the fact that if you don't study for your English test then um, yeah, you're going to do pretty badly. So next time – study for it.

A lot of really successful people will tell you that it was their failures that ultimately led to their major successes. Failure makes you work harder for your goals. And long-term success is all about hard work.

It pays to be persistent

A great example is my friend and fellow Australian author Kate Morton. It wasn't until she was in her mid-twenties that Kate decided she wanted to be a novelist. So she wrote her first novel. Nobody wanted it. She tried again and wrote a second novel. Guess what? Nobody wanted that one either. Refusing to give up on her dream of being an author, Kate sat back down at her computer and wrote a third novel. That book, *The Shifting Fog*, has been published in 29 countries around the world and has sold more than one million copies. Today, Kate Morton is considered to be one of Australia's brightest literary talents. But best of all, thanks to Kate's resilience and persistence, she now earns a living doing what she loves.

Kate Morton's advice about failure ...

An elderly friend of mine used to say that you should make lemonade from lemons. I knew what she meant, but it took me a while to fully understand that the best thing about failure is that it always makes you better at what you do. From failure comes knowledge and it's your job to make the most of it, to channel it into determination to do better next time.

And if you're doing something that you really love, a bit of failure along the way won't stop you from doing it some more. Keep your eye on the prize, but learn to love the journey. I'd have kept writing whether I was published or not. (In fact, I did keep writing despite being knocked back – repeatedly – by every major publisher in Australia.) And when I look at my earlier unpublished manuscripts, I breathe a huge sigh of relief. Even though I was devastated at the time, I can see now that they simply weren't good enough and, if they had been published, my writing career would have had a totally different shape. Besides, with each failure I got a little closer to achieving my dream: my first manuscript won me an agent, the second a reader's report from a big-time publisher, before the third, finally, scored a publishing contract, wee-hah!

I know it's cold comfort while you're floundering in the sour fug of rejection, but failure gives your life and your work texture – a story – and it makes success, when it comes (and it will come if you just keep going), all the sweeter. Just like lemonade.

I wasn't born a world-champion, I just worked really hard to become one.

Layne Beachley, seven-time women's world surfing champion

A few of my biggest mistakes, biggest disappointments and most embarrassing moments ...

- Despite the fact that I attended a co-ed school, nobody asked me to my year 12 formal. So I asked one of my older brother's friends (who I had secretly loved in a somewhat stalker fashion for many years). He agreed to go with me, sprained his ankle on the day and spent the entire night sitting at the table. The worst bit? The next day he asked my best friend out on a date. Needless to say, I was gutted. But you know what? I got over it.

- Despite playing netball for many years I failed to even make it onto the C-grade netball team in year ten. In revenge, I formed a D-team and we played anyway, even though our results weren't formally recognised in the school competition.

- When I was in high school I desperately wanted to be a children's TV host, so I would write away to the TV stations begging for auditions. I failed every single one of them. At the time I was devastated. Little did I know I would end up being a published author instead!

- I failed my manual driver's licence test twice before giving up and switching to automatic. Fifteen years later at the age of 34 I decided to try again for my manual licence. Guess what? I failed again. Refusing to give in, I went for one more manual test a few months later and finally passed with flying colours!

3 Your feelings are your inner compass

Ever felt seriously confused when you've had to make a decision? Well here's a tip: your feelings are sort of like your own personal GPS, an inner compass guiding you on which direction to take.

Some people call it:

* **their gut instinct**
* **tuning into their feelings**
* **their inner voice**
* **their intuition.**

Whatever you call it – the key is to pay attention to it.

If you've got a choice to make and one of them just feels wrong then it's probably a good indication that you shouldn't go in that direction. And it could be anything. Maybe you're deciding whether or not to go to a certain party. Maybe it's about taking a part-time job you've been offered. Maybe it's about taking a short cut home. Maybe it's about trusting someone you hardly know or someone you do know or your parents know who gives you a bad vibe. When your gut instinct gives you a niggling feeling that something is wrong, when you get a bad vibe from a person or a situation, when you feel suddenly uncomfortable around somebody – listen to it. Your instincts are rarely wrong. Even if the person giving you the bad vibe is a family friend – it doesn't matter. Listen to your gut instinct and stay away from that person.

We've all got a sixth sense (not an I-see-dead-people sixth sense, but an *intuitive* sixth sense) and if you can learn to tap into it, it will pretty much always alert you to bad situations. The key is to learn to get quiet and pay attention to your feelings.

Even Oprah says she follows the 'When in doubt – don't' rule. If you're not sure about something, wait until you get some clarity. How do you get clarity? Sometimes you get it by finding out more information or by asking the opinions of people who don't have a vested interest in the answer. Sometimes it's about not rushing into a decision on the spot when you're feeling pressured. Instead, talk to family, your friends or someone else you trust.

Of course, sometimes you feel like your gut instinct is telling you not to do something when it's really just your anxiety or paranoia talking. So you've got to try and learn to distinguish the difference. Your intuition or gut instinct is usually a strong feeling that won't go away no matter how much other people try to convince you otherwise. And there's a difference between feeling anxious about getting up to sing karaoke and feeling scared about getting in your best friend's boyfriend's car.

Remember – when you're on the right path it feels really good. You can still feel nervous or excited but you shouldn't get an uh-oh feeling in the pit of your stomach. If you feel uncomfortable, that's your instincts telling you to stop and choose a different path.

Which brings me to the notion of red flags. Here's what I know. Life waves big, red flags at you when you're on the wrong path. There are always warning signs that you're heading down a street that, frankly, you really don't want to be on.

So pay attention.

In short: go with your gut.

When the world is noisy I close my eyes and breathe, I take stock of that gut instinct and get through the chaos. I know only my true self awareness can navigate the bombardment of choices and advice. Only I can walk the path.

Tara June Winch, writer

Recommended reading:
The gift of fear

One of my favourite books on this subject is *The gift of fear* by world-renowned security expert Gavin de Becker. In his book, de Becker discusses how powerful our gut instinct is in alerting us to potentially dangerous situations. Women in particular are raised to be polite and not to hurt people's feelings. What this means is that when a guy stops us on the street and asks us for directions or asks for a lift or offers to carry something to our car for us, even if he gives us the creeps or makes us feel uncomfortable, we don't like to say 'no thanks' in case we hurt his feelings. But as de Becker points out, girls and women don't get attacked because they were mean to a guy. More likely, girls and women get abducted, raped or worse because they were *too nice* – by that I mean they allowed men to get into their personal space even when they thought the guy was creepy and weird. A guy may be good looking, he may be totally charming, he may even be a family friend but he may still give you the creeps for some reason. If that happens, pay attention to your feelings and get the hell out of there. Better to be safe than sorry.

4 You don't have to be sporty to walk the dog

I'm going to give it to you straight – you need to make friends with exercise during your school years. In primary school and even early high school, you may be pretty active. As a kid I did ballet, played tennis, netball and a bit of tee-ball, rode my bike, roller-skated up and down our verandah and routinely spent my afternoons running around the neighbours' backyard dressed in swimmers and high heels playing Charlie's Angels. (I successfully arrested my dog 834 times.)

As a high school student I ditched all of that and spent my time sitting at my desk pretending to study but really plotting ways to get a guy called Brendan to fall madly in love with me.

You see, somewhere along the line in high school, many of us drop physical activity faster than you can say, 'I hate my thighs. Do you think Brendan knows I'm stalking him?' Maybe, like me, from year 10 onwards you couldn't get into any sporting teams at school. Maybe you or your parents thought you should focus on your studies. Or maybe the thought of playing sport just makes you gag. Whatever the reason, it doesn't matter. The thing is you need to get active for at least thirty minutes every day.

So you don't like sport? That's totally fine. Doing regular exercise has nothing to do with being sporty. Turn to the back of this book and have a glance at me as a teenager. Do I look even remotely sporty? (Rhetorical question, no need to answer.)

Find something. Anything. How about:

* walk the dog every afternoon
* go for a run in the mornings
* jump rope
* rollerblade
* take a dance class
* join a gym
* mow the lawn
* play tennis
* play a sport on your Wii
* do an aerobics DVD in the privacy of your own home.

It doesn't matter – the key is to get your heart pumping.

When I was in my senior years of high school I was what you would call chubby. I did no exercise (apart from the compulsory PE class twice a week which I often attempted – and usually failed – to wag) and I have to say I was fairly miserable about my appearance. I would look at the girls in the basketball and netball teams, the girls who rowed or went to swimming training and I was totally envious of them and their physiques. I thought they were born *lucky* and I was just *unlucky* because they were sporty and I wasn't. Looking back, I can see that was a ridiculous way to look at it. The truth is I could've been just as fit as them if I'd gotten off the couch and actually done something. Okay so I wasn't sporty, but as I've said before, you don't have to be sporty to exercise.

These days I either go for a walk or a run a few times a week, I try to play indoor netball once a week with some friends and I do an hour of weight training once a week with a personal trainer. And while I don't always love exercising, I love what it does for me. It makes me feel fit.

Repeat after me: exercise is my friend

* When you exercise, your body releases happy chemicals – endorphins. Ahhh. We love endorphins. That's the chemical that's also released when we're in love or eating chocolate or staring at a photo of Hugh Jackman (or maybe that's just me). That's why exercise is also a great tool in treating depression. Studies show exercise can even be as effective as antidepressants. So if you're feeling a little blue, strap on your shoes and go for a thirty-minute walk. I'll bet you feel better.
* Exercise helps improve your focus and concentration at school. Many doctors say it will also help you sleep better.
* Exercise is a great way to de-stress and unwind. I love taking my dog Chewie for walks in the mornings. That's when I think about the day ahead. I find the walk really meditative – in other words, I tend to chill out when I go for a walk in the fresh air.

The skinny on being skinny

Exercise should not be about trying to become a size 4 or even a size 8. Hello? You're not meant to be a human Bratz doll. And if you think guys will like you better the skinnier you are, think again. In 2008, men's magazine *FHM* conducted an online survey of 60,000 men presenting them with three bikini-clad models: a size 8, a size 12 and a size 14. Four out of five guys chose the size 12 or size 14 girls as their favoured body shape.

Some girls seem to become obsessed with being skinny. According to the Eating Disorders Association, approximately 2–3% of young Australian women suffer from the eating disorders anorexia or bulimia. Having an eating disorder can be life threatening. Sufferers can wind up with permanent health problems including kidney dysfunction, infertility (which means they can't have a baby) and brittle bones to name a few. If you think you might know someone with an eating disorder, encourage them to talk to an adult about it.

What if you're naturally slim? That's okay. Just make sure you eat well (lots of fruit, vegies and lean protein) and don't live on junk food.

The key is to take good care of the body you have. So exercise for you. Exercise because you want to be fit and healthy. Exercise because it will make you feel better. Enough said.

In short: move it, sister!

5 Not even Miranda Kerr always looks like Miranda Kerr

As a teenager I was desperate to look like Madonna. Trust me, back in the 80s Madonna was the hottest rock chick on the planet. She was 24 years old, releasing songs like, 'Lucky Star' and 'Borderline' and her fashion sense (consisting mainly of black lace, crucifixes and crop tops) made her seem daring and cool. Naturally, I copied her style only to wind up looking like a slightly slutty nun with bad shoes. (Thank you, Dunlop Volleys.)

So my point is this: desperately wanting to look like the models, actresses and celebrities that fill the pages of magazines is nothing new. In the 1950s nearly every young girl wanted to be Marilyn Monroe. In the 80s everyone wanted to be Madonna or Molly Ringwald or Susanna Hoffs from The Bangles. In the 90s it was all about Gwen Stefani and Kate Moss. Today you're more likely to want to look like Beyoncé or Miranda Kerr. I bet in fifteen years a whole stack of teenage girls will be wishing they looked like Beyonce's daughter.

Sadly, trying to look like our favourite celebrities is completely pointless. Unless you're willing to have serious plastic surgery it's just not gonna happen. Plus the cold, hard truth is that not even Miranda Kerr always looks like Miranda Kerr. I'm sure if Miranda were here right now she'd tell you the same thing.

That's not to say that Miranda or Beyoncé weren't born naturally beautiful. Some people (a very, very, very small percentage) were just born with amazing proportions and bone structure – it's like they won the Looks Lotto. But those pics that you and I stare at in *WHO*, *Girlfriend* or *Vogue* aren't exactly real. They're highly crafted images. An entire team of people has been working on those images for a number of hours to create that look.

On every photo shoot there's at least one hair stylist,

a highly trained make-up artist, wardrobe consultants – and that's before the model puts one elbow in front of the camera. Lighting, certain angles and poses are also used to create the illusion of perfection. And don't get me started on airbrushing. Once that photo is taken there's somebody sitting at a computer editing the image. Centimetres are magically brushed off thighs, legs can be lengthened, zits and blemishes magically disappear. Don't believe me? Google the words 'Kate Winslet *GQ* airbrushing' and you'll read about how Kate magically had her legs lengthened and thinned out for the cover of *GQ* magazine a few years ago. In September 2009, a US health and fitness magazine called *Self* airbrushed a cover image of Kelly Clarkson so that she was literally half her real size. What the – ?

Even better is the now famous Dove commercial. Type 'Dove Evolution Commercial' into Google or YouTube (or go to www.dove.us) and you'll see the entire before and after process from make-up and hair to airbrushing and the finished billboard. Check out how they lengthen the model's neck.

And don't think celebrities aren't the same. From Angelina Jolie to Miley Cyrus, these people have stylists and make-up artists on call choosing their outfits, doing their hair and making sure they look a million bucks before they step out the door.

Believe me, if you or I had access to the 'people' the celebrities have, we'd look pretty hot too.

I'm guessing you know this stuff already but sometimes it's good to be reminded that comparing yourself to Miranda Kerr is only going to do your head in and make you feel really bad about yourself. I bet there are days when Miranda Kerr wakes up and wishes she looked like Miranda Kerr ...

Confidence, baby, confidence

So, you wanna be able to turn heads when you walk into a room? Who doesn't? Confidence is the key and it comes from within. If you feel gorgeous, if you know deep in your soul that you're 'all that', then that confidence radiates from you. Girls who are confident in their own skin, who aren't trying to look or be something they're not, are the ones other people are attracted to. How do you get confidence? It's all about having high self-esteem and a healthy self-image. You need to know you're gorgeous both inside and out.

I was horribly awkward and felt very uncool all through school. I remember my first week of school in Australia when I was watching another girl eat a Sunny Boy (frozen drink) and thinking 'I wish I was cool and blonde like her and not Chinese with black hair and not an utter dork.' It didn't help that I flipped open my lunch box that day to discover chicken giblets braised in soy and star anise. Yes, a favourite from my great aunt, bless her, thinking she would provide all the things I love for my first day at school. What have I learnt since then? As you grow, whatever makes you feel different is also what will set you apart as a unique individual later in life. Learn to like yourself and have faith that if you are kind, generous and empathetic, people will find you beautiful in ways beyond the physical.

Poh Ling Yeow, artist, cook and MasterChef 2009 finalist

How to feel gorgeous on the inside ...

* Behave in a way that makes you feel proud of yourself. Always act with integrity and kindness.
* Be a great, loyal friend.
* Don't spread gossip and don't bitch about others – you'll only feel worse about yourself afterwards.
* Think about doing volunteer work occasionally (more on that on page 69).
* Know that you have something special to offer the world – there is no one quite like you on this planet.
* Be kind to yourself. Monitor your self-talk (that's the voice in your head) and make sure it is 80% positive and only about 20% critical. So if you're telling yourself, 'I'm a loser' fifty times a day, that's no good for your self-esteem. When you find yourself bullying yourself in your head, change your self-talk to something positive like, 'I'm a great friend' or 'I have fantastic taste in music'.
* Instead of focusing on your faults, concentrate on what you're good at and things you love about

yourself. Maybe you're artistic, maybe you're seriously good at science, maybe you have fabulous curly hair or a smile that lights up a room or really beautiful hands. (I bite my nails so I always admire other people's lovely hands.) Whatever it is, congratulate yourself on it and keep going.

* Write up an affirmation chart and list 5–10 things that are great about yourself (see above). Read that list out loud to the mirror every day and mean it!

How to feel gorgeous on the outside ...

* Take care with your appearance. Consider doing a deportment and grooming course to teach you how to look after your hair, nails and skin.
* Exercise regularly so that you feel fit and healthy.
* Eat lots of fresh fruit and vegies, lean protein and wholegrain foods and don't shove junk food in your gob every day.

* Drink plenty of water (to keep your skin clear) and stay out of the sun (to ensure your face doesn't resemble an old leather handbag when you're thirty).
* Get at least eight hours of sleep a night.
* Don't smoke – it gives you wrinkles around your mouth and turns your teeth yellow.
* Learn what colours and styles suit you. Don't be a fashion victim – understand that the latest styles and colours may look horrendous on you. Express your creativity and individuality through your clothes!
* Okay, so you're short and curvy or tall and skinny with no curves at all! Find your best feature (your lovely green eyes, your long neck, your luscious hair, your elegant hands) – and flaunt it! You are beautiful just as you are! Make the most of what you have and remember that beauty comes in all shapes and sizes.

It's a shame that as women we're so prone to compare ourselves – to images and to each other. The images you see in magazines are almost entirely contrived. With every passing year, more and more technology is developed to make more and more digital changes to the photographs that you see to the point where women often now look like plastic space aliens. Seek out magazines who represent women in a way you can relate to and don't for a moment think that even the models look like that in real life. They don't.

Mia Freedman, former editor of *Dolly*, *Cleo & Cosmo* magazines, see www.mamamia.com.au

In short: discover your inner goddess.

6 Your future success has little to do with your year 12 score

Some things have certainly changed since I left school. But there's one thing which hasn't changed: this idea that your final leaving score when you finish year 12 dictates the rest of your life. The pressure was there when I was at school and it's still there today. For some reason, many teachers, school career counsellors and parents want you to believe that how well you do in year 12 will determine the rest of your life.

That's a HUGE amount of pressure and, frankly, it's wildly inaccurate in my opinion.

Your future success is not determined by your high school grades or by one single event like your year 10 grades or your year 12 leaving score. For starters, think about Sir Richard Branson – he didn't even finish high school. Even Einstein apparently failed French. On the flip side, there are some students who top every subject at school, gain the highest possible leaving score, win much-coveted university places and go on to fail miserably at life. In other words, an impressive final leaving score is no guarantee of future success in the same way that bad grades don't mean you're doomed to be an eternal failure.

Now before you start cheering 'Rebecca Sparrow says that grades don't matter!' while simultaneously trying to set fire to your school books as your parents search for the number of their lawyer, let me say this. The reason you should want to work hard and get good grades at school is so that at the end of year 12 you have choices. The better you do at school, the more options you'll have when you leave. And options are always a good thing. And whatever career or job you want – florist, designer, mechanic, doctor, actor, teacher, hairdresser – you will most likely need some formal training or qualifications behind you. Keep that in mind.

I should point out that I didn't get the final score I needed to get into the communications degree I desperately wanted to do when I graduated from high school. After I got over my total devastation I realised I could just do the degree part-time and then after two years I could upgrade to full-time study. For the record, not one single employer to this day has ever asked me what my final score was. Not one.

So work hard at school, do your best so that you have no regrets but don't go thinking your whole life is over if you don't get the leaving score you need or expected. After all, I didn't and I turned out okay.

Score? What Score?

The traditional high school path doesn't suit everyone. Maybe you're planning to leave school after Year 10 to do an apprenticeship or learn a trade. Or maybe you're going to stay at school but go down a vocational learning path. What's smart is doing what works best for you. Just ask Virgin Airlines founder, Sir Richard Branson ...

I had a teacher at high school – we'll call her Mrs Brown for legal reasons. I told her I wanted to be a comedian and she said, 'You are not funny and you are never going to be funny'. So when we were doing *The Glasshouse*, I always said I wanted it to be called, 'Stick it up your arse, Mrs Brown'.

Wil Anderson, host of *The Gruen Transfer*

Don't stress too much about high school. There's always time to make up for it. I failed everything but English in my senior year. But 15 years later, I won a University Medal for academic achievement at the University of Queensland and was winning awards for my fantasy novels. Some of us are just late bloomers, and that's perfectly okay. The most interesting people in the world are often those who achieve things in roundabout ways, later in life, after they've lived a little.

Kim Wilkins, author

When I was in high school, I wish I'd known not to get down just because I couldn't clearly see how I was going to become the successful woman of my dreams. In high school I had short hair and a face full of pimples. I used to think to myself, 'How can someone that looks like me ever be a successful fashion designer?'. I wish I had known that dreams really can come true. Always imagine yourself in the best possible situation – negative thinking will get you nowhere, but positive thoughts will get you everywhere. Don't forget to dream, it gives you something to aspire to. If you forget your dreams, you often lose your way.

Juli Grbac, designer (winner of *Project Runway* 2008)

So you don't know what you want to do?

Join the club! A few people are lucky enough to know exactly what they want to do when they leave school but for most students it's a bit of a mystery. And that's totally okay. The key to choosing a career is following your passion. Not your parents' passion. Not your Gran's passion. Your passion. Follow your passion and you'll wind up with a job you adore which hardly feels like work at all.

Ask yourself:

* **Is there something I absolutely love? (Okay, other than Liam Hemsworth …)**
* **What am I good at?**
* **What topic could I talk about all day?**
* **If anything were possible, what would my dream job be?**

Drawing a blank? Not even sure how to answer those questions? Don't panic. Ask your friends or parents what they could see you doing. (If your parents say, 'Doing the washing up, for starters', then perhaps ask an aunt or cousin.) You could also think about seeing a professional career counsellor – they're often fantastic at helping to pinpoint great career choices. At the very least they'll give you a few ideas to start thinking about. Or maybe you need to take a break from study and go travelling for a year. Travel always helps broaden your outlook and opens you up to experiences you may never have had otherwise. It may also be just what you need to help clarify which direction you want to take.

Keep in mind you're not just likely to change jobs many times, you'll actually change professions a number of times during your working life. New research indicates that Generation Y and Z (that's you!) will change careers five times (if not more) in their life. FIVE! What the – ? Life is about trying different things, so don't go thinking that whatever you choose at the end of school is what you have to do for the rest of your life.

In my current group of friends, only one person has stayed in the same career. My friend Nicola studied journalism, ended up working in marketing and is now back at university part-time training as a speech therapist. My friend Kat spent ten years working as a high school science teacher but is now back at university studying to be a pharmacist. My partner Brad left school to become an accountant, then after two years he went back to uni and studied to become a journalist. He worked as a journo for a few years and then went back to uni to study medicine. He now works as a doctor. My pal Mandy left school and trained as a hairdresser but these days works in government usually in the area of sports and recreation since she's a sports nut. As for me? I studied communications and originally worked in public relations. I spent a few years working as a magazine editor and now I work full time as a novelist and newspaper columnist.

So if your high school grades don't dictate your success in life then what does? Your attitude.

You will become what you believe

Your future depends on you, how hard you're willing to work and your attitude towards life. If you can stay focused on your goals, are resilient when confronted with failure, have a self-belief that you always land on your feet and have an enthusiasm and energy to succeed then I believe you will. You will find a way to achieve your goals – no matter the obstacles in your path. Sometimes you may need to adjust your goals along the way. And sometimes you need to be flexible about what those goals should be. I spent years agonising over working in TV. Was that really meant to be my path in life? No. (Perhaps the fact that I failed every single audition was a clue. Hello?) Now I know that I was meant to be a writer – it just took me a while to realise it.

In Australia, as compared to many second and third world nations, we live in a country that is full of opportunity and freedoms. Here you can wear what you want, say what you want, vote for who you want, travel where you want. A primary and high school education is available to all and there are a myriad of resources and services available to help those in need of a helping hand. So really, the majority of limitations you're going to face in your life are ones you can choose to overcome.

That's why I believe that in life you will become what you believe is possible for yourself. If you walk around believing you're not smart enough, talented enough, focused enough, tall enough, pretty enough or rich enough to fulfil your dreams and goals then – most likely – you won't. If you give up at the first sign of difficulty, if you throw in the towel at your first taste of failure, then chances are you'll get nowhere.

Mental as anything

I'm a big believer in the power of visualisation. It's something athletes regularly use to help them achieve their goals. A good example is Beijing Olympics gold medallist for pole vault Steve Hooker. Not only did Steve train incredibly hard, in interviews he often talks about how he used visualisation techniques to help him sail to gold in the Bird's Nest stadium.

In an interview with Jessica Halloran which appeared in the *Sydney Morning Herald*, Steve said of his visualisation strategy, 'I felt like that kind of stuff was cool. The more you do it the more you realise pole vault is mental. Just having any sort of mental stimulation, where you are thinking deeply about what you're doing, helps.'

Similarly, former Australian paralympic swimmer Karni Liddell claims that a positive attitude is what saw her confounding doctors who told her she wouldn't live past her teenage years (see Karni's quote on page 62).

Of course, sitting around visualising yourself with a dream job, or acing an exam or working as a model or sailing over a 5.8m high bar in the Olympics pole vault final isn't going to be enough to make it happen. You MUST put the work in. Take active steps towards your goal, study hard, train or do work experience and use visualisation and positive thinking as an added tool.

I was born with a muscle-wasting disease called spinal muscular atrophy. My parents and I were told by many specialists that I would not crawl, walk or live past my teenage years. Most doctors told my parents to make me as comfortable as possible as exercise would only make my condition worse! I was very fortunate to have amazingly determined parents who used their common sense and decided to spend every minute of their lives improving mine and they realised that for me to have a great life I had to be healthy, happy and positive. I have no tricep muscles and limited leg muscles. I cannot lift my arms above my head and I have limited lung capacity yet all I have ever wanted to do was do the most physical thing you can ever do in your life. I wanted to be an elite paralympic athlete. Well, I broke my first world record in swimming at the age of 14. In 2000 I went into the Sydney Paralympics as the fastest female swimmer in the world for all my events. But I had more dreams. I wanted to be a journalist and a model. I have achieved both those goals and even worked as a commentator at the Athens Paralympics.

The hardest part of your journey to success will be telling people your crazy dreams and ideas. But I've found as soon as you say your dreams aloud, many people will come to your side and help guide your journey in the right direction. During my 30-year journey living with my disease I have discovered that you will always be surrounded by help, support and light if you stay positive in spite of hardships.

Karni Liddell, journalist and paralympic bronze medalist

The girl most likely?

In February 2000 I was unemployed, broke and living at home with my parents – at the ripe old age of 27! That's when I decided I was going to have a career change. I was going to write a novel! Some friends were supportive of the idea but others looked at me as though I had rocks in my head. 'You haven't even studied creative writing,' they pointed out. 'And do you know how hard it is to get published in Australia? Don't get your hopes up.'

I had read the grim statistics on how hard it was to get a publishing deal in Australia but I was determined to give this new career my best shot. So before I even started writing my novel I went to the newspaper and cut out one of those Top Ten lists of books. I liquid-papered out the name of the book in the number one spot and then I went to my computer and in the exact same font I typed my name and the name of my novel. Then I printed it out and stuck it to the top of the list. So now I had a Top Ten list of books with my name in the number one spot.

I put that list next to my laptop and I looked at it every day I was writing. Every morning, before I sat down at my computer, I started to spend five minutes visualising walking into a bookstore and seeing a book on the shelves with my name on the cover. When friends found out what I was doing they thought I was a bit loopy but I didn't care – I kept working on my novel and imagining myself succeeding. Three years later that novel was in bookstores. *The Girl Most Likely* spent sixteen weeks in the local Top Ten including four weeks at number one. It has been reprinted about five times. Better still, I sold the film rights and hope to turn my novel into a movie!

In short: write your own success story.

7 Give back and gain perspective

When you're in the thick of what seems like a crisis it's easy to blow things out of proportion. You humiliate yourself in front of your classmates, you fail an exam you expected to pass, you get dumped, your parents refuse to let you go to a certain party or for the fifth time in a row you fail a TV screen test even though you thought you interacted really, really well with the snake puppet. (Okay, so that last one might just be me.) All of these experiences can feel incredibly painful.

But sometimes it's worth remembering that, well, things could actually be worse. Having to stay home instead of going to a party is not actually the end of the world. It might feel like it at the time but in the scheme of things, in the big picture, it's not so bad.

One way to keep things in perspective is to try and incorporate volunteer work into your life. After all, if you have a roof over your head, access to clean water whenever you want, plenty of food to eat and you get to go to school and get an education, then you're ahead of hundreds of millions of people.

Did you know ...

- 963 million people go to bed hungry every night. (www.amnesty.org.au)
- One billion people live in slums. (www.amnesty.org.au)
- More than 150 million children between 5 and 14 years of age are engaged in child labour. (www.unicef.org.au)
- Approximately 93 million children are not in school. The majority are girls. (www.unicef.org)
- 105,000 Australians are homeless every night. (www.homlessnessaustralia.org.au)

How you respond to those sorts of facts is up to you. But in many ways you could say that as a young person who lives in a first world country, who has access to education and health services, food, water, clothing and shelter, as someone who can without a doubt go on to fulfil their dreams, you have a responsibility to make the most of the opportunities given to you. In other words, you have no excuse not to dream big, work hard and go for it.

You could also decide to make sure that every year that goes by, at least one person breathes easier because of you. Volunteer work is a great reminder that there is always someone out there who is struggling more than we are. It helps put your own problems in perspective. You'll also feel really good about yourself afterwards. Making a difference in the life of another person is easier than you might think.

So what are you waiting for?

You could:

* Go through your wardrobe every season and decide to donate the clothes you no longer like or wear to a women's and children's shelter.
* Encourage your school community to donate new pairs of woollen socks every June to Mission Australia or other charities who care for the homeless. Blankets and socks are two of the items most in need.
* Choose a charity or two every year and door-knock or fundraise for them.
* Gather together friends and family members and make dinner for the families who are staying at your local Ronald McDonald House because their children are in hospital.
* Sponsor a child overseas through World Vision or do the Forty-Hour Famine.
* Offer to do the weekly grocery shopping or walk the dog of an elderly person you know.
* Use your skills (maybe you're a great artist, really good on the computer or a superb cook) and donate your time to a local not-for-profit organisation.

Redefining success

It's easy to assume that being successful in life means earning a huge salary, living in an expensive home and wearing designer clothes. It took me a few years to realise that the people who I considered to be really successful were the ones who were working in a job they loved, who were giving back to the community and who had great relationships with their friends and family.

Twenty years ago my room was covered in posters of Johnny Depp and Kirk Cameron. Today, I admire people like Jamie Oliver, Oprah Winfrey, Dr Catherine Hamlin and Sarah Murdoch. My role models today are people who combine their passion in life (chef, TV host, doctor model) with community service. They have found ways to use their skills to give back to the community and make a difference.

In short: lend a hand.

When I was in high school I wish I had known that there were many ways to learn, and being at school was just one way. Often it is the lessons we learn outside the school room that are the most valuable.

Every school holidays I worked in my parent's medical practice. I would meet people from all walks of life, young and old, some battling terminal illnesses. I remember one day at the end of year 12, meeting a young woman my own age afflicted by motor neuron disease. She couldn't run and play like I could. Her courage and strength made me put my own teenage problems into perspective and reminded me just how lucky I was to have my health, my family and a future unencumbered by illness.

Throughout high school, I wish I had known the importance of noticing others and allowing their experiences to enrich my own life. Other people's stories and experiences will inspire you to learn, to change, and to evolve.

Elizabeth Broderick, Sex Discrimination Commissioner and Commissioner Responsible for Age Discrimination

8 Binge drinking can make you look really stupid (and smoking gives you yellow teeth ...)

Oi! This chapter deals with alcohol, drugs and smoking. You may want to talk to your parents before you read any further. Or you may not feel ready to read this stuff just yet. On the other hand, if you're currently sitting in a chair wearing a smoking jacket, puffing on a cigar and nursing a glass of port, read on ...

Let's be realistic. Experimentation with alcohol is seen as a normal part of the teenage experience. But let me say this. Binge drinking is incredibly risky. Not entirely sure what I mean by 'binge drinking'? It means drinking a lot of alcohol really fast. The official definition of binge drinking is consuming more than four standard drinks in two hours.

At best, when you binge drink you run the risk of looking completely ridiculous in front of your friends. You might spew everywhere, pass out, act like a complete tool or do something with someone you will completely regret.

At worst, when you get drunk you're putting yourself in enormous danger of sexual assault, car accidents, theft, pranks and verbal and physical fights. When you're intoxicated (drunk), your intuition and ability to think clearly is at an all-time low, and you find yourself making decisions and doing things that you wouldn't normally do. Your radar (alerting you to potentially dangerous or creepy people or situations) is way off. In short: when you're hammered you become an easier target. Let's be clear, though, that the victim is NEVER TO BLAME. Full responsibility lays with the perpetrator who chooses to take advantage of someone who is in a vulnerable state.

All that pretty much turned me off binge drinking at school. I guess I was too obsessed with my image, but I already felt completely uncool and I didn't want to be the subject of gossip. Not that I'm an angel. I had a number of binge drinking episodes in my twenties which resulted in me falling down a flight of stairs in front of everyone at a bar in London, trying to walk (unsuccessfully) down the street and falling into a pile of garbage on the side of the road and ringing ex-boyfriends to discuss why our relationships failed (naturally I just made myself look like an enormous drunken desperado). Another time, my flatmates and I held a massive 1960s themed party but I drank so much so quickly that I passed out by 9pm and missed the entire thing. Loser.

If you're feeling pressured to drink, there are a range of strategies you can use:

* **Carry around a softdrink with you all night (no one needs to know you're only drinking lemonade).**
* **Tell people you're the designated driver for the evening.**

* Tell people that after one drink you seem to develop the IQ of a squid and would prefer not to end up taking off your knickers and shaving your head at this party.
* Tell people you have to be up early in the morning for work or some family thing or for training and that you don't want to be hungover.
* Tell people you're not feeling well and the thought of drinking alcohol makes you want to vomit.
* Now, maybe you don't want to go to a certain party in the first place. My tip? Develop a code word with your mum, a sister or a friend. That way when you ask your mum for permission to go to a party (which you really don't want to go to), you can use your code word and your mum will know to say, 'Sorry, you can't go. We're visiting your grandparents that night.'

If you've decided to completely ignore my advice and are thinking 'Bugger it, I'm getting smashed anyway', then at the very least have friends around whom you can trust. Have your drinking session at home where (a) you can make your own drinks and (b) you can safely vomit in your own bathroom and still climb into your own bed. You might want to have one sober friend with you as well, since you're going to need someone to hold your hair back while you're vomiting into the toilet. If you're going out, eat something before you leave home, try to drink a glass of water in between every rum and coke, keep an eye on your drink at all times (so it's not spiked) and organise for one friend to be the designated driver. Most important of all – make a pact with your pals that you all leave the bar/club/party together. No exceptions.

Your Brain + Alcohol = Bad News

Teenage brains are still developing. So what? So even one alcoholic drink can do your still-growing-teenage-brain some damage. That's why medical experts now say there is *no safe or recommended amount of alcohol for a teenager*. Put off trying alcohol for as long as you can – until you're at least 16. And don't even think about getting drunk until you're over 20 when your brain has fully grown. And what about the long-term consequences of regular binge drinking? Excessive drinking can lead to liver damage, stomach ulcers, infertility, high blood pressure, strokes and certain cancers. Nice.

The pole dancing lesson ...

When I was in year 10 there was a huge party that pretty much everyone in my grade attended. I was never a big drinker but I carried around a West Coast Cooler (a very popular alco-pop in the 80s) and sipped on it in an attempt to fit in. What I remember most about that party though was that one of the girls from school got totally blind and wound up doing some kind of pole dance/striptease thing in the garage in front of everyone. Then she passed out with one of her boobs hanging out of her top. At school on the Monday she was the number one topic of conversation and her image was ruined for a loooong time. Trust me when I say that when you binge drink – as a teen or as an adult – you run the risk of people laughing at you and gossiping about you behind your back. At the time, when you're smashed, you'll think you're the life of the party and that everyone thinks you're hilarious. Believe me when I tell you that they're more likely laughing AT you, not WITH you. And that's the last thing you really want to happen.

As for smoking ...

Without fail every single adult I know who smokes is trying to quit. True. In fact, speak to any adult smoker and they will most likely tell you that taking up smoking is one of their biggest regrets in life (closely followed by wearing parachute pants and waistcoats in the 80s). Why? Smoking can kill you (lung cancer, anyone?) and it's incredibly expensive. From an image point of view, smoking causes stained, yellow teeth, bad skin, wrinkles and stinky breath.

You probably know that cigarettes contain nicotine, which is highly addictive. But did you know that you don't have to smoke every day to become addicted?

Many students experiment with cigarettes at some point. I did. I clearly remember the day I had some school friends over when one of them pulled out a pack of cigarettes and we all had one. Thankfully, I couldn't stand the taste or the sensation of smoke rolling down my throat. On top of that I hated the fact that smoking left you with gross, stinky hair and even stinkier clothes. I also thought that kids who sat around bum-puffing looked incredibly lame and I didn't want to be viewed that way. And from a purely materialistic point of view, I worked really hard at a part-time job at Myer for my spare money and I wasn't about to spend my hard-earned cash on cancer-sticks. Hello? That money was going to go towards clothes, music and an overseas holiday to the UK.

Even though I'd made the decision that smoking wasn't my thing, I still remember feeling a little stressed when I was offered cigarettes at parties. How did I swerve my way around it? I lied. A lot. A number of times I said I had asthma and wasn't allowed to smoke (COMPLETE LIE). Other times, I said that I'd given up (COMPLETE LIE and clearly an attempt to look cool by me). But what shocked me the most, I guess, was that even when I was offered cigarettes and told the truth by saying, 'Nah, I'm not into it', people seemed fine with my answer. Maybe this is because I was leaving more cigarettes for them! I don't know, but all of these approaches worked for me.

What about the illegal stuff?

Let's start with cannabis. Also known as marijuana, pot, dope, mull, weed, grass, Mary Jane, ganja, reefer, spliff, Buddha – this drug has more aliases than P Diddy! Essentially, cannabis is a depressant drug. That doesn't mean it will make you depressed, it means they slow down the functions of the central nervous system.

Now some people will say that smoking the occasional joint (marijuana cigarette) isn't going to do you any damage, it's just going to make you feel really relaxed and chilled out (or 'stoned'). But at the risk of sounding like your mother, let me point out that (a) smoking cannabis is actually illegal and (b) it *can* trigger depression and anxiety, particularly in young women. Be aware that it is possible to become addicted to cannabis and frequent and heavy use can make you totally paranoid and/or seriously forgetful and really, really, really BORING. You should also know that in some rare cases, smoking marijuana – even once – has triggered mental illness including schizophrenia. For the latest information on marijuana and its effects go to the National Cannabis Prevention and Information Centre website www.ncpic.org.au.

As for harder drugs (stuff like speed, ice, coke, ecstasy and heroin); don't even go there. You risk losing your money, your mind, your friends, your family and, ultimately, your future. Do you really want to end up looking like Amy Winehouse? I rest my case.

If you're still not convinced, remember this: if you get caught with an illegal drug of any type, you can be charged with a criminal offence. A criminal record means you can kiss goodbye a variety of careers including lawyer, teacher, police officer, diplomat and worst of all, you'll never get to be Miss Universe.

If you or someone you know is having issues with smoking, alcohol or drug abuse, turn to page 118 for websites and services that can help.

In short: just say no.

9 Love is meant to feel great!

There's no love more exciting than first love. Secret crushes. First kisses. The total butterfly-in-the-stomach excitement you feel when you find out the person you like actually – oh my God! – likes you back!

But how can you tell how someone really feels about you? Well, it's easier to work out than you might think. Stop listening to what they say when you're together and pay attention to what they do. In other words, judge their *behaviour* not what's coming out of their mouth. Anyone can be charming. Anyone can flatter. But real love is how somebody treats you. And I'm not talking about whether or not they give you flowers or buy you presents. How do they treat you as a person?

Ask yourself:

* **Do I feel good about myself when I'm with them?**
* **Do they treat me with respect?**
* **Do they call when they say they're going to call?**
* **Do they care about my feelings?**
* **Do they want to spend time with me even if we're just going to the movies or walking around the shops?**
* **Do my parents and friends like them?**
* **Are we able to have long conversations about all kinds of stuff?**

If you can answer yes to all of these questions, they could be a keeper!

Unconditional love is a myth!

Talk about being brainwashed. Hollywood has been spewing out movies and music for years on this idea of unconditional romantic love. It's the notion that no matter what happens, no matter what someone says or does, you will always love them.

Well, you know what? That's a big, fat lie. While your parents can love you unconditionally, romantic love needs conditions. There should be certain deal-breakers in relationships like if they:

* hit you or threaten you
* regularly put you down, call you stupid, call you fat or make fun of you
* call you bitch, slut or whore or anything equally demeaning (this is sooo **not** okay)
* cheat on you
* want you to lie to your parents about stuff

* **start trying to control you by telling you what to wear, where you can go and who you can see and talk to**
* **pressure you to do anything you don't want to do (take drugs/have sex etc).**

You need to enter relationships with a high level of self-respect, knowing your self-worth. If someone wants the privilege of dating you, then they need to treat you the way you deserve to be treated. Someone who calls you bitch or slut does not respect you. Neither does someone who pressures you to do things you don't want to do, or doesn't care about your feelings. So if your boyfriend/girlfriend does any of the above or worse, then dump them. END OF STORY.

Hold it right there!

The following information deals with sex. It's pretty full on. So if you're under 16, you may not feel ready to read this section just yet. Or you may want to speak to your parents before you read it. But if you **are** thinking about having sex, read this chapter before you do ANYTHING ...

I will not do it in a car, I will not do it in a bar ...

Sex. You know we had to go there. Today there's more pressure than ever before to lose that virgin tag faster than you can say, 'But that only lasted forty seconds'. It may seem like EVERYBODY is having sex but the truth is, they're not. According to the *Fourth National Survey of Australian Secondary Students, HIV/AIDS and Sexual Health 2008*, 27.4% of year 10 students have lost their virginity. So that means that a whopping 72.6% of year 10 students are still virgins. So if you're still the Big V, you're not alone.

Exactly when you should start having sex is an issue you need to *really*, *really* think about. Take it seriously. Before you have sex for the first time, think about getting some advice and talking about the pros and cons: you could go to your parents, family doctor, youth group leader or school counsellor. And what about religious beliefs? Are you religious? Does having sex before you are married go against everything you believe? You may want to keep that in mind too. There's lots to consider. For what it's worth, here's my opinion on the whole teen sex issue.

* Don't even think about having sex until you're at least sixteen – the legal age. Having sex is a big deal and comes with lots of physical and emotional consequences. You could get pregnant. You could get a sexually transmitted infection. You could have sex with a guy who you later find out loves to sing Delta Goodrem songs at karaoke bars in his spare time. All stuff to think about.

* There's nothing wrong with being a virgin. And just because you reach the legal age to have sex, it doesn't mean you have to. You may be ready or you may not. When it comes to having sex the most important thing is that you feel respected and safe.

* Any guy who says he'll dump you if you don't have sex with him is going to dump you anyway. Any guy who says he'll dump you if you won't give him oral sex is going to dump you anyway. No decent guy would EVER say that to a girl he seriously liked and respected.

* Similarly, any guy who says he'll only date you if you have sex with him is only ever going to use you for sex. Any guy who says he'll only date you if you perform oral sex on him is only every going to use you for oral sex. He has no intention of being your boyfriend. If he calls you a prude or a tease, hand him the Yellow Pages and tell him to go look under H for hooker.

* There are guys out there who will say whatever they have to say and make promises they have no intention of keeping just to get sex.

* Most adults will tell you their first kiss is a way better memory than that of the first time they had sex.

* Remember, in real life sex is NOTHING like online porn. NOTHING. Sex is not meant to be degrading or painful or humiliating. It should be as much about your pleasure as your partner's. And just so you know, the first time you have sex is usually pretty awkward and may even be a bit physically painful.

* I would also suggest you and your partner have a full sexual health check from your local GP or family planning clinic before you do anything. If you're not careful, you'll have a lasting reminder of your first sexual experience ... it's called herpes.

* The idea that oral sex doesn't count as sex is ridiculous. Oral sex is a HUGELY intimate activity. And did you know you can get sexually transmitted infections from oral sex? Yep. We're talking chlamydia and gonorrhoea in your throat and herpes in your mouth. Any guy who regularly pressures you into giving him a blow job (oral sex) is using you. When it's one-sided, the act becomes totally sexist and demeaning.

* Never ever EVER have sex without using a condom. Unless of course you want to run the risk of getting pregnant or catching a sexually transmitted infection. YIKES! In fact, if you're going to have sex you should have TWO forms of contraception ready. If the first condom breaks, have another one within easy reach. That way you won't be tempted to have unprotected sex.

* No means no. And you don't need to give a reason. 'No' is a complete sentence. If you say no to any type of sexual activity and someone forces themselves on you then that's called SEXUAL ASSAULT. (This includes date rape – where you are forced into sex or a sexual act or a sexual act is done to you by someone you know or were on a date with.) You can go to the police and they can be charged. Remember that consent has to be gained right through the experience.

  So you may say YES at the beginning, you may say YES in the middle but you can still say NO at ANY TIME when you want to stop.

Some not-so-sexy facts

* There is a huge range of sexually transmitted infections you can get from having vaginal, anal and oral sex. Believe me when I tell you, pregnancy is not your only concern. Some of these STIs can kill you (AIDS/HIV). Others can ruin your chances of ever having children. And others will just leave you really, well, itchy. Many STIs have no symptoms and some of them – like herpes – can keep coming back even once you get rid of them. The most common sexually transmitted infection amongst young people is chlamydia which can cause infertility.

* Condoms can prevent many sexually transmitted infections but not all of them.

I kissed a girl ...

It's really, really common to go through a phase when you question your sexuality. Maybe you have a girl crush on a female teacher because you admire her so much. Or maybe, like the Katy Perry song says, you kissed a girl and didn't find it half bad. Trust me, there's more to being gay than pashing another chick. For starters, you have to like listening to the Indigo Girls. (Okay, that was a bit of lesbian humour there ...)

But let's say you do think you are gay – then what? Don't panic. There are lots of places you can find support, chat to other gay teenagers and get advice. A good place to start is www.twenty10.org.au.

If you're feeling a bit confused, your first step should be to find a non-judgemental friend to talk to about it. And you will find one. I've known my best friend Kaz since we were five-years-old. We went through primary and high school together. She's an awesome singer, makes fantastic pesto pizza, owns way too many pairs of shoes and is one of the messiest people I've ever lived with. She's also gay. Big deal.

Sex, lies & videotape

A quick word about sexting (the current trend of sending naked or semi-naked or pornographic images or suggestive text via mobile phone).

Please listen to me when I tell you this – a picture lives forever. FOREVER. If you take a photo of yourself and email it to another person, you will have no control where that photo ends up and it could haunt you for the rest of your life. Any guy who tries to convince you to be filmed having sex, or any guy who tries to convince you to send him naked photos is NOT THE GUY FOR YOU. Trust me. When it comes to sex and your naked body be camera shy. From a legal point of view, if you have naked photos of someone under the age of sixteen on your phone or computer, you could be charged with having child pornography. Try explaining that to a future employer. 'In my spare time I like going to the movies, playing netball, oh and about two years ago I was charged with having child pornography on my laptop ...'

online

...you're on the internet all the time. I know you've probably visited chat rooms and started chatting to complete strangers. Just be aware that Jason, that hot 17-year-old you think you're talking to is probably a 45-year-old man called Frank who looks like Homer Simpson and smells like bad BO.

The internet is NO PLACE to find love. Chat rooms are full of paedophiles – most often adult men pretending to be teenage boys (or sometimes girls) and they groom you for up to six months. That means they'll email you for up to six months pretending to be the world's best boyfriend or girlfriend. Then you agree to meet them in person and guess what? The scene is like something out of *Wolf Creek* (world's scariest movie about a serial killer). Don't be fooled. If you're desperate to find love, pester your mum to let you go to school dances. Do a drama class on the weekends. Or develop a love for paint-ball or skirmish (you may get shot, so be prepared to look cute with paint on your face).

In short: respect yourself.

I was a teenage desperado …

One flick through my teenage diaries and it's pretty clear how desperately I wanted a boyfriend. After all, girls who had boyfriends seemed incredibly cool. Even if a girl was a bit of a geek, she gained a new respect in everyone's eyes if she had a boyfriend.

As a teenager with pretty much no romantic prospects (I blame the perm), I was totally in love with the idea of being in love. The thought of having a boyfriend who would send me flowers and cards, who would spend his time confessing his undying love for me, who would hold my hand as we walked around the mall and who would accompany me to school dances and formals was all I could think about. Well that and working as a children's TV host.

I never really had a boyfriend at high school and – guess what? – neither do lots of other girls. Considering most high school relationships (a) only seem to last about three months and (b) are full of drama, tears and arguments, it's quite possibly a blessing in disguise that you're a single girl about town. Relish it. What I know now is that high school can actually be waaaaay more enjoyable if you stay single. Crushes are great fun. So are first kisses. But you've got the rest of your life to have a serious boyfriend. So chill out. Enjoy your freedom. Hang out with your tribe and unless a fabulous guy comes along – fugeddaboudit.

10 Just Ask!

Okay, this final lesson is short but big. **Ask**. **Ask** for advice. **Ask** for help. **Ask** for a second opinion. **Ask** to get clarification. **Ask** when you're unsure. **Ask**. **Ask**. **Ask**. I wish I'd known in high school that there are many, many people who are willing to lend you a helping hand and all you have to do is **ask** for help. That's the truth.

You don't need to suffer and struggle alone. Don't be afraid to ask someone for advice or help if you're:

* having problems at home (maybe your parents are going through a divorce or you're not getting on with your mum or your new step-parent)
* struggling with a particular subject at school
* being bullied by other students
* confused about a school assignment or a project
* worried about one of your friends or a member of your family

The truth is that most adults love to give advice. Sad but true! And most people are really happy to help you out. So if you approach a friendly teacher, a school counsellor or pastor, one of your relatives or a family friend all you'd have to say is, 'I was wondering if you could help me with something ...' or 'Can I get your opinion on something ...'

Sometimes, when you're at school, it can feel like you're all alone as you struggle to keep your teachers, your parents and your friends happy. It can be a really confusing time too and the last thing you want is to be stressed – or more stressed than you already are!

So never be afraid to put your hand up and ask for help. And if the first person you ask (like a particularly cranky teacher) says no, go ask someone else instead. Help is out there, I promise.

I asked a few friends of mine (aged between 18 and 65) for some advice about surviving high school. Here's the advice they wanted to pass on to you ...

I wish I'd known that who you are in high school is not who you have to be for the rest of your life. High school is often about labeling people. You're the sporty girl, or the goody-goody, the loner, the gossip. It doesn't matter. The fact is, once school is finished you get to reinvent yourself. Hold on to that.

Rebecca

It's impossible to hunt down and destroy everyone's copy of the yearbook. Look your best on the day your year 12 photo is taken.

Kate

Go for the quiet guy. He's much less likely to break your heart.

Laurie

Be nice to other girls, don't let competition turn ugly. Support friends. Funnily enough, that's what friends do.

Bronwyn

Two bits of advice from me ...

1. Try not to let everything build up – your emotions or schoolwork. If you are feeling overwhelmed or upset, sometimes your friends aren't always the best people to talk to, remember they are only teenagers too. Find someone you can confide in. It doesn't have to be the school counselor but a teacher or adult you can trust. A problem shared is a problem halved. Being able to talk to someone privately who isn't directly involved will help you immeasurably throughout high school and life.

2. Two words will shape your high school experience: Get Involved. You will not look back and say, 'I'm glad I didn't do that'. You will look back and wish you had. Don't worry whether it's cool or not – becoming involved in your school not only gives you friendship and life skills, it makes you a leader.

Laura Gartry

2008 high school graduate,
Hawker Scholar 2009

I wish I had known that everything works out okay even when you are convinced that this time it really is a disaster. Things that seem huge now will fade. You will be amazed at how much you can do, create, endure and survive. I wish I had known to worry less and enjoy more; to be less inhibited by fears and to be open to everything. I wish I had known that my internal struggles and worries actually meant nothing; they were simply an uncomfortable, intangible inner experience that didn't have to have any impact on anything outside of me. What's really important is what you do and how you are with others. My advice is: don't wait to feel comfortable before taking on challenges because this may never happen – pick up your discomfort and take it along for the ride.

Clare

When I was in high school I wish I'd known that listening was so important! Actively listening to someone when they talk or share something with you means that you can understand at a deep level what the conversation or topic is about and it is the key to remembering that information at a later date.

Belinda

When I was in high school I wish I'd known that there was something called feminism out there. I didn't understand until I reached university two years later and read *The Women's Room* by Marilyn French.

Jessica

The only person whose approval you need is your own. Run your own race.

Alexandria

I wish I'd known that my crush for my entire school life would 20 years later ask me to marry him. Life is about timing.

Natalie

I wish I'd known that when you finish high school all the people you had around you for the last 5 years really do go their own way and you have a whole lot of friendship building to do at uni if you don't bother to keep in very regular contact.

Tanya

I have four pieces of advice ...

1. You can't do it (high school) alone. You need to find friends, people who share the same interests and will 'have your back'. That sounds almost gang like but you need at least one other person who will stick up for you. Someone to laugh at your jokes other than yourself.

2. Get involved. Sport, drama, school council, whatever floats your boat. Instant group of friends. You don't have to be awesome at it, either. There's a role for all personality types.

3. Get a part-time job. If you can manage school and work it gives you a chance to meet new people outside of school (especially members of the opposite sex, which is very important if you go to an all girls school) – and you don't have to rely on your parents for income.

4. There are always going to be people in the world who will try to make you feel unworthy or bad about yourself. They make themselves feel superior by making someone else feel inferior. In high school this is called 'bullying'. Unfortunately, it doesn't always stop in high school. It can and will happen throughout life in various ways – your boyfriend, your workmate etc. They only have power over you if you give it to them. Easy to say, not always easy to do.

Rowena

I wish I'd known why I was there at all. It wasn't until three years after year 12 that I actually worked out what I wanted to do with my life. The rest is history. I also wish I had had a better understanding of who I was as a person and known that being wrong/incorrect at school isn't a reflection of whether you will be right/wrong in life. A teacher's opinion in assessing a piece of work is only their opinion.

Robbie

I wish I'd known that the people you didn't get along with you'd probably never see again in your life, so it wasn't worth stressing about them.

Belinda

I wish I'd realised that what the cool kids were doing wasn't actually that cool. And that being unique was a good thing.

Diana

When I was in high school I wish I'd known that it doesn't last forever. As a kid, those six short years from year 7 to 12 seemed to stretch on and on into infinity, and the infiniteness of it all served to heighten the intensity of the good times and the bad. With the benefit of 20 years' hindsight I can see the fantastic learning experiences that even those bad times offered – even if I didn't appreciate them at the time!

Justine

When I was in high school I wish I'd known of the law of attraction – that what you focus on becomes your reality. Wow, that would have been powerful!

Paige

When I was in high school I wish I'd known that things DO get easier and the mistakes you make, fights you have and broken hearts you nurse will become life lessons that you look back on as a key part in shaping who you become as an adult.

Rebecca

Three things from me ...

1. When I was in high school I wish I'd known to take myself less seriously! During my senior years I dedicated a lot of my time to study (and spent less time doing the things I loved like acting and theatre). While I achieved great results, I realised later on you're only a teenager once and school is certainly not a live or die situation!

2. Study, have fun and immerse yourself with things/people or hobbies that excite you and make your OWN light shine! School is tough, so make sure you have a hobby that creates a balance in your life. If you're doing the best YOU can do, and having fun in the outside world, that's all you, your teachers, or parents can ever ask for.

3. I haven't as yet used my high school grades or been to university (like I had planned to at school), however I am riding the wave of a challenging and exciting acting career. I have learnt a positive, open-minded attitude far outweighs an OP grade or an A on an assignment!

Kendal Rae

actress and former tv presenter on *The Shak*

When I was in high school I wish I had known that we are all different and in knowing that, loving who I am would have been so much easier! And I wish I had known that teachers are humans too!

Mia

When I was in high school I wish I'd known that future success wouldn't depend on looks, but more on personality and drive.

Maren

When I was at high school I wish I'd known more about the world and felt empowered about how to help it. Maybe I'd have been a little less self-absorbed and found my place in that wider world a little more easily.

Kate

When I was in high school I wish I'd known that the prayer, 'Dear God let Brenda and Jackie be my friends forever' would come true. Because then I would have taken a photo of their Bay City Roller outfits to show their gorgeous daughters one day.

Melina Marchetta

author

Other stuff ...

There is, of course, a whole list of other stuff I want you to know. Like how important it is to find a mentor in the field of work you want to get into, that you should learn how to budget and understand the traps involved with using credit cards, that it's important to start at the bottom when you get a job, that you should listen to your teachers when they tell you to plan out your assignments before you do them and that having good table manners can take you into any situation with confidence. And, if you have to lie on your bed to zip up your jeans – they're TOO TIGHT!

Recommended reading

Girl stuff: your full-on guide to the teen years

Kaz Cooke

This book is a one-stop shop for everything to do with being a girl. From dealing with zits and family problems to finding your first job and learning how not to get ripped off when you go shopping, this guide deserves a place on your bookshelf!

The gift of fear: survival signals that protect us from violence

Gavin De Becker

Learn how recognising fear and trusting your gut instincts can save your life.

I've read the rules, now how do I play the game?: guidelines for the game of life

Vicki Bennett

One of my favourite books which helps teach you skills like positive thinking and visualisation.

Life smart: choices for young people about friendship, family and future

Vicki Bennett

A really practical book to help you survive the teen years that includes advice on friendships, finding your direction, self-belief and relating to your family.

Change the world for ten bucks

Install green lightbulbs, bake a cake for a neighbour, learn CPR – small things can make a big difference in your community.

Surviving year 12: a sanity kit for students and their parents

Dr Michael Carr-Gregg

The ultimate guide to surviving the pressures and stresses of year 12! You'll know Dr Michael Carr-Gregg as the agony uncle in *Girlfriend* magazine and from his regular appearances on *Sunrise*.

Recommended websites

For your head ...

www.reachout.com

This website offers practical help and guidance on a huge range of issues including depression and suicide, relationships, smoking, drugs, pregnancy, eating disorders and lots more. From the privacy of your own home you can get the facts from a reliable source.

www.bullyingnoway.com.au

If you're being bullied or are doing the bullying, go to this site for practical advice and support.

www.cybersmart.gov.au

A government website offering tips on how to deal with cyberbullying and other online hassles and traps.

www.kidshelpline.com.au

Trained counsellors are there to listen to your concerns and offer you great advice. Free counselling is available online, by email or over the phone by calling 1800 551 800.

www.twenty10.org.au

This website is specifically for teenagers who feel confused about their sexuality and feel that they may be gay. An excellent, supportive site!

www.thebutterflyfoundation.org.au

The Butterfly Foundation is an organisation which gives advice and support to people who suffer from eating disorders. If you think you might have issues with food or know someone who does, this site is a good starting point.

www.likeitis.org.au

Another great website giving you the facts on puberty, peer pressure and sex. All facts. No rubbish.

www.somazone.com.au

An Australian website offering free, fast, anonymous access to health questions and answers. Somazone is a program of the Australian Drug Foundation (ADF).

For your heart ...

www.dove.us

The Dove website is fantastic and helps bust some of the myths in the beauty industry. This is where you'll find the Dove Evolution commercial which shows the entire process a model goes through in a billboard campaign. Watch how they extend her neck and plump up her lips in the editing process! Click on 'Features' then click on 'Videos' and you'll see the one marked 'Evolution'.

www.girlwithasatchel.com

Former Deputy Editor of *Girlfriend* magazine Erica Bartle writes this daily blog about fashion, magazines and more. Bartle's strong Christian beliefs ensure the site is savvy but not bitchy. An excellent destination for fashion addicts. Erica's motto is 'the good behind the gloss'.

www.meetmeatmikes.com

How I love this site! I'm rather hopeless at making things but Pip Lincolne (who writes this blog from Melbourne) talks about all the cool things she makes by hand and gives you tips on how to do it, too. I especially like the brooches she makes out of domino tiles and the Little Golden Book purses!

www.madeit.com.au

If you are handy with a needle and thread (or a glue gun and a jar of sequins), maybe you can make a few dollars selling your homemade stuff online. Beats flippin' burgers.

www.insideadog.com.au

If books and words and great stories and amazing characters make your heart sing, this site by the State Library of Victoria is where you should go. There are interviews with authors and lots of discussions about books. If you love books, you'll love it!

www.dumbofeather.com

Now this website is brilliant. Read the magazine online or buy it at a newsagent. Either way, each edition profiles five extraordinary people who are creative and passionate and inspiring. When you're searching for a bit of inspiration, Dumbo Feather is click-worthy.

www.rebeccasparrow.com

And finally, visit my website if you have any feedback, suggestions or questions.

Here's what I looked like in high school:

Acknowledgements

Back in 2006 I started talking to Madonna Duffy about this book. I had no idea what shape it would take but Madonna was enthusiastic and supportive and did a good job of pretending not to be concerned in the slightest that technically I was meant to be writing a different novel at the time! As always, thank you MD.

Thanks to the gorgeous Kristina Schulz for her wisdom, kindness and author-friendly approach – you are a delight to work with, KS! Thanks to the glorious Christina Pagliaro who brought so much to this book, not just in the editing but in providing insights into life as the parent of a nearly-teenage girl and for being unphased when Ava and I crashed her office to correct page-proofs. And to my evil twin Meredene Hill – you're the triple threat baby!

My dear friend Jean Yates provided encouragement and fabulous feedback right along the journey and I am indebted to her and the 2009 class of 8D at Ipswich Girls Grammar who were the world's best test-market when it came to preliminary titles and covers.

Similarly, clinical psychologist Dr Clare Rosoman generously gave her time to read through several versions of this book, giving feedback and advice. As did Sarah Gawthorne who cast her eyes over the manuscript and offered valuable suggestions. Thank you.

It wasn't until I was pregnant with my daughter Ava that I felt inspired to finally turn this book into a reality. So I thank Ava for her patience (I edited chapters in between rounds of Baa Baa Black Sheep), I thank Chewie for being such a good listener on our walks and I thank my husband Brad for his tremendous love and support. And finally, I thank my parents who steered me through my high school years with love and patience (particularly on the day I came home with multiple piercings in my ears. Sorry about that ...)